A HAPPY ENDING BOOK ™

First Day at School

by Jane Carruth   illustrated by Tony Hutchings

MODERN PUBLISHING
A Division of Unisystems, Inc.
New York, New York 10022

One morning Chippy went shopping with his mother. He soon found a box of his favorite cereal. But Mommy said, "Put it back, Chippy. We do not need that today."

Chippy was very surprised when he heard his mother ask Mr. Acorn where he kept the workbooks, pencils and crayons.

"At the far end of the store," said Mr. Acorn, smiling. "Well, well, I suppose you're getting Chippy ready for his first day at school!"

"I don't want to go to school," Chippy said, as they left the store. "I don't want pencils and crayons and workbooks. I want potato chips and some of Mr. Acorn's candy."

Mommy shook her head as she hurried along. "You know it won't be long before you go to school," she said. "And you will need all these things." But Chippy still looked angry and upset as he followed Mommy indoors and watched her put the things she had bought for school in the big chest in her bedroom.

The next day Chippy was riding his tricycle in the garden when his friend, Susie, came along. "Can you come and play?" Chippy asked. "Mommy is too busy to take me out."

Susie hesitated. "I could," she said at last. "But not for long. My Mommy is taking me shopping to get a new dress for my first day at school."

Chippy made a face. "I'm going to hate my first day at school," he said. "Anyway, let's go into the house. Mommy is in the backyard so we can play by ourselves. I've got something to show you."

Chippy took Susie upstairs. "I'll show you what's inside the big chest in Mommy's room," he said. "Follow me!"

Susie helped Chippy raise the heavy lid. Then she gasped. "All these things are for your first day at school, Chippy!" she cried.

"I guess so," said Chippy. Then he took the new workbook and began tearing out the pages.

Chippy and Susie were having a good time drawing funny faces on the torn out pages of the workbook when Mommy found them. No wonder she was angry! "You will just have to take your ruined workbook to school," she told Chippy.

The very next Monday Chippy left for school. He wore
his new striped T-shirt and he had a new school bag and a
big blue lunch box which was a surprise from Daddy. "I wish
you looked happier," said Mommy, as she hurried him along.

Susie was standing beside the teacher when they arrived. And Mommy said quickly, "I'll leave you now . . ."

Poor Chippy! He looked so miserable that the teacher called out, "Come and stand by me, Chippy! You can ring the school bell."

"I-I don't want to," said Chippy in his sulky voice.

"I do, I do!" Susie cried. "I want to . . ."

"No, you don't," said Chippy. "I'll ring the bell." And he took the big bell and swung it up and down.

"Well done, Chippy," said the teacher, smiling.

It had been fun ringing the big bell. But once inside the classroom, Chippy began to feel miserable again. When the teacher gathered the others around her to listen to a story, Chippy refused to join in. And when he turned his back on her, she pretended not to notice.

But Chippy couldn't help hearing the story and, at last, ever so slowly, he moved towards the others. Soon the teacher was asking, ''Who knows what happened next?''

''I know!'' said Chippy. ''Old Grunter fell over.'' Everybody clapped and the teacher said, ''Very good, Chippy.''

"You were clever about the story," Susie whispered, when they sat down to their morning snack. Chippy laughed. Then he opened his brand-new lunch box and found his favorite cookies.

To Susie's surprise, when the teacher asked someone to sweep up the crumbs, Chippy put up his hand. "I thought you hated school," she said softly.

"Oh—well—now I feel different," Chippy murmured. "I just wish I hadn't ruined my workbook."